Frog I  ner

CW00857727

Margaret Eleanor Leigh

Animals of the Valley # 1

ISBN-13: 978-1502385925
ISBN-10: 1502385929

Chapter One

"There's not an uglier dog in the whole of Wales," the chief Pound Officer said at least once a day. He would stand in front of the kennel that housed the dog called Frog and pull a long face.

Frog did not think it was a useful comment. It did not do his confidence any good, and it wasn't even true. How could the chief Pound Officer know there wasn't an uglier dog in the whole of Wales? It wasn't as if he had *seen* all the dogs in Wales.

"Don't tell me that dog is *still* here!" was the other comment Frog hated nearly as much.

"Trouble is, no-one wants a dog that looks like a frog," the assistant Pound Officer would reply. "I *try* and get people to take a second look at him, but it's the first look that does the damage. I mean, let's face it, would *you* want a dog that looked like that?"

For Frog was in truth one of the ugliest dogs ever to be housed in Merthyr Vale Dog Shelter, and there had been some really ugly dogs over the years. He was the size and shape of a very large beach ball and his skin rolled down his back in loose uneven folds. He had short stumpy legs and a tail the shape of a small rudder from a boat. His round head was too large for his body, and his eyes could barely be seen beneath rolls of frog-like facial skin. To top it off he had two small sticky-up pig ears.

Frog turned his back on the Pound Officers. He didn't like being talked about as if he wasn't even there, and as if he couldn't understand. And he didn't like the things they said about the way he looked.

"What are we going to do with him?" the chief Pound Officer said one day, after Frog had been with them two months. "We can't keep him here forever."

A cold shiver ran up and down Frog's rounded spine. He didn't like the sound of that at all.

"I suppose we could feature him as *Dog of the Week*," the assistant Pound Officer said, pursing his lips doubtfully. "It's probably a waste of time, but we could give it a try."

Frog spun round. His pig ears went up; his wrinkled frog face was wreathed in smiles; his tail swirled. He looked like a Martian about to ascend into space.

For Frog knew *exactly* what happened to dogs featured in the *Dog of the Week* advertisement. They *always* got a home. People came from all over Wales to adopt the *Dog of the Week*.

The *Dog of the Week* went to exciting places like Cardiff or Swansea or Tenby. Why, just the other week a spaniel had gone to the beautiful village of Laugharne. Frog had drooled with jealousy over that.

"Ugh, look at that revolting dog slobbering in that kennel," said the boy of the family that adopted the spaniel.

"Ewww," said the boy's mother with a shudder, glancing at Frog before turning back to the spaniel, and saying in a silly high voice: "Come to your new mummy, Puppy Pudding."

Frog knew no-one would ever call him Puppy Pudding. But if truth be told, and Frog always tried to be truthful, he didn't specially want to be called Puppy Pudding. It was just not dignified. He just wanted to be loved for his good qualities, and of those he knew he had plenty.

It was Frog's big day — the day he was to be bathed, groomed and photographed for the *Dog of the Week* advertisement. *Dog of the Week!* He could scarcely believe his luck.

It was even worth the terribleness of being bathed. Frog hated being bathed. The temperature of the water was never right — it was either too hot or too cold and the shampoo always found its way into places where shampoo had no right to go.

Frog bore it all patiently. No gain without pain, no gain without pain, he told himself over and over, trying not to yelp when the shampoo made his eyes sting. If the *Dog of the Week* advertisement worked, he may never have to be bathed by the Pound Officers again.

When they'd finished—and they seemed to take forever—his short brown coat shone like a bright new penny. There was just one problem. Nothing else had changed. He'd just gone from being a dirty frog to a clean and shiny one. For no amount of bathing and brushing was ever going to make Frog look like anything but a giant frog.

"It's a miracle we need," said the assistant Pound Officer. "Only a miracle will make this dog look good in his photograph."

"We could try photographing him by candlelight," grinned the chief Pound Officer. He spent a lot of time fiddling about with the viewfinder on his camera trying to find a good angle.

"Maybe just shake the camera a bit so the picture comes out blurred," suggested the assistant Pound Officer helpfully. "That's probably our best chance." He pulled out a notepad and pen. "Now we have to describe him."

"Well, good luck with that," said the chief Pound Officer.

There was a long silence while the assistant Pound Officer chewed the end of his pen. He was having a lot of trouble finding words to describe Frog.

"*Last hope for a dog called Frog,*" he said at last. "That would make a good heading. It should tug at a few heart strings, and that's what we want, isn't it?"

Frog thought it sounded dreadful. What if his last hope failed? What would happen to him then? He would have preferred something snappy and positive, like *Once in a lifetime opportunity to adopt the incredible dog called Frog.*

"Just put something general and more-or-less true," said the chief Pound Officer at last. "How about *lovable, good-natured dog, ugly, but with a heart of gold*?"

Frog's heart of gold swelled up a little at that. How true, he thought. How true. He was willing to overlook what they said about him being ugly, because he thought the stuff about the heart of gold was more important.

Then the Pound Officers argued for a while about the sort of dog breed Frog might be. Eventually they decided to leave that bit blank, because he was like no other dog they'd ever seen.

At last it was done, and there was nothing left for Frog to do but wait for his new perfect dream family to walk through the doors of Merthyr Vale Animal Shelter. Then they'd whisk him away to a perfect house in a perfect town to enjoy a perfect new life.

Chapter Two

Lots of people saw the *Dog of the Week* advertisement in the newspaper, and on Saturday, which was Open Day at the shelter, there came a steady stream of people, all planning to adopt Frog. The blurred photograph and the heart-stirring caption had done the trick nicely.

Then everything turned to custard. "He's not quite what we had in mind," they'd murmur, one by one, and they'd start looking at dogs in the other kennels instead. Lots of dogs in the other kennels were adopted that day, but no-one wanted Frog.

It was all very upsetting, and Frog had to fight hard not to cry. Time was running out, Open Day was drawing to a close, and his last hope was slipping away.

But then came the Joneses. Frog decided at once they wouldn't do at all. They just weren't his type. Mr Jones was round and balding with a large red face and a loud checked shirt that didn't quite meet across his belly. There were gaps between the buttons where his skin poked out.

Mrs Jones was very thin, with a worried expression, a faded blue cotton dress, and a mop of untidy faded brown hair. Then there were the three young Joneses: two boys and a girl, all three scruffy-looking and loud and all talking at once. No, the Joneses were not Frog's cup of tea at all.

"Oy, but he's an ugly-looking mongrel of a dog," said Mr Jones, staring at Frog through round blue eyes.

"Well, we knew that," replied Mrs Jones. "That's why we chose him, remember? He's ugly, but he has a heart of gold. That's what the advert said."

"Yes, but the photograph didn't tell the whole story, did it?" Mr Jones thought the photograph had been most misleading. Plain untruthful, in fact.

Frog stared back at Mr Jones. He didn't think Mr Jones was much of an oil painting either.

But fair play to the Joneses. It did not cross their minds to go home without Frog. It was Frog they'd come to adopt, because was Frog was on his last hope. They hadn't come for any other dog, and they weren't about to leave with any other dog, even though there were plenty of others to choose from.

There was a long moment that seemed to stretch on forever. The Joneses stared at Frog and Frog stared back at the Joneses. The two Pound Officers stood quietly behind the counter, scarcely daring to breathe.

"Orwight," said Mr Jones, turning away from his long study of Frog. "He'll do. So what happens now?"

"You're taking him?!" The assistant Pound Officer could not believe it.

"Aye, of course we're taking 'im," Mr Jones said impatiently. "That's what we're 'ere for, ain't it?"

"You hear that Frog?" shouted the chief Pound Officer joyfully, "You've done it! You've got yourself a new home. At last!"

I'm not deaf, thought Frog, *there's no need to shout.* He wasn't even excited. This was not the sort of family he'd had in mind. They weren't at all smart for one thing. They dropped their "h's" a lot, and said "'ere," instead of here, and "'ome" instead of home. Frog's dream family did everything perfectly, and that included speaking perfectly. Frog's dream family was the sort of perfectly shiny family you see on television. But now it looked like he was stuck with the Joneses instead.

Mr and Mrs Jones went to fill out forms at the counter while the three Jones children fought each other to pet Frog.

"Let me smooth him!" yelled the small Jones girl, whose name was Bethan. She was seven and she had untidy mousy brown hair that looked as if it hadn't been brushed in a while and big blue eyes. All the Joneses had big blue eyes.

"No! Let *me* smooth him. It's *my* turn now, you've already smoothed him twice," shouted Miles, who was nine. He was very thin and had knees and elbows knobbly as golf balls. Bethan and Miles both looked like miniature Mrs Joneses, for she was also all bones and sharp sticky-out bits.

"Oy, out of the way, it's my turn," roared the older Jones boy. Euan was an eleven-year-old version of Mr Jones—just as short, round, and red-faced.

All the racket they were making made Frog's ears hurt. Still, he'd not been petted much before in his lonely life, and the "smoothing," as they called it, felt surprisingly pleasant. Frog thought he might even grow to like it. His little rudder of a tail twitched with pleasure in spite of himself.

"Look at his tail," squealed Bethan. "It's just like a pig's tail!"

"No, it ain't," said Euan, who never agreed with anything Bethan said, on principle.

"Yes it is," shrieked Bethan.

"No it ain't. Pigs have curly thin tails. His is short and fat and flat."

They went on and on, arguing about his short, fat and flat tail, until Frog felt so self-conscious he sat down on it, to hide it.

At last the forms were filled in. It was time to say goodbye to the Pound Officers who had looked after him, and to the kennel that had been home for the last two months.

"Bye, Frog," said the chief Pound Officer, beaming with relief. "Be a good boy. We don't want you back here next week, do we?"

Frog could think of nothing he wanted less either.

The Jones' car was old and brown with lots of dents and scratches. It made a lot of noise and sounded unwell. Frog was squashed between Bethan and Euan on the back seat. Bethan put her skinny arm around his wide shoulders and Frog felt his heart swell a little. Was this what happiness felt like?

"What do you reckon Monster will do when he sees Frog?" Miles asked as the old brown car farted and burped its way out of the car park and headed in the direction of the Heads of the Valleys road.

"Try and eat him, probably," said Euan casually.

Frog stiffened. Monster? Monster? He was to be eaten by a monster? *Help*, he screamed silently. *Help!*

"Monster will just hate him," said Mrs Jones with what sounded to Frog like an unfeeling laugh. "At least at first."

Frog peered out of the window at the rolling Welsh hills and the narrow valleys and trembled inwardly at the thought of an unknown monster waiting at the Jones' house, all ready to eat him.

At Aberdare, Mr Jones turned south along the Cardiff Road, and into the Cynon Valley. It was a narrow snaking valley that followed a narrow snaking river, and it had steep sides dotted with a scattering of hillside villages.

"Welcome to the Cynon Valley, Frog," Mr Jones said. "I hope you will be very happy here."

Perhaps Mr Jones wasn't so bad after all, Frog thought, in spite of keeping a monster at home. They'd now reached the village of Cynon Bach and very striking it was too. It wasn't at all pretty, but it was dramatic. It was set in a steep and narrow switch of the valley, so narrow it was really little more than a ravine. On the one side was a wooded mountainside, and on the other there were rows of houses curving up the hillside like rows of stone seats in an outdoor theatre, reaching almost to the very top of the hill.

That was where the Joneses lived — on the topmost row of houses. The little old car puffed and panted and almost came to a halt in its struggle to get up the hill.

"That dog must weigh a ton," grumbled Mr Jones, glancing in the rear view mirror at the largeness of Frog. "It ain't normally this much trouble getting the car up the hill."

Frog thought that was a bit rich, coming from Mr Jones.

They pulled up outside a very narrow three-storey miner's cottage, bang in the middle of a long row of identical houses. It seemed everything was narrow round here. The houses were narrow, the street was narrow, the valley itself was narrow. The only things that weren't narrow were Frog, Mr. Jones, and Euan.

Frog and the Joneses tumbled out onto the pavement. At once, all along the street, people's curtains started twitching, because that's what people's curtains did every time something new happened in Cynon Bach.

"You'd think folk would have something better to do than watch out for other folk's business," tutted Mrs Jones. "Look at Dulcie Morgan over there, peering out at us, bold as brass. It'll be all over the village by tea-time that we've got us a new dog."

Mrs Jones unlocked the front door, and Frog padded cautiously into his new home and looked around him curiously. It was shabby ("lived in" Mrs Jones called it), but it was clean, and it was homely. It was the sort of house a dog could relax in. He could imagine himself stretched out on the threadbare living room carpet, watching the lives of much shinier families on television along with the Joneses. He could imagine himself curled up with the children on their untidy beds.

Frog plodded gravely round the house. It might even do, he thought, it might even do very well. Suddenly he found he didn't mind anymore that it wasn't perfect and shiny, like those homes on television. He wouldn't have to worry about ruining things, because there was nothing to ruin.

"Show Frog the garden," Mrs Jones called, "I'm sure he will like it."

Because the house was so narrow, each floor had just a couple of narrow rooms. On the top floor were three tiny bedrooms, on the ground floor the living room and a small dining room. In the basement was the kitchen and a bathroom, and a door that opened onto a narrow and steeply sloping garden. It was small, but it was filled with flowers and sunshine.

The day was warm and summery, with clear skies and there was a gentle breeze rolling in from the south. From the valley floor below, there rose up a wonderful mix of smells for Frog to enjoy.

He liked the garden very much indeed. It had a high wooden fence all round and above that there was a view across the valley to the wooded mountain on the other side. But it wasn't the view that caught Frog's eye: it was those flower beds. Oh yes, those flower beds were a bit of all right — just perfect for digging.

Frog took a few steps into the garden and tested out the soil for diggability. It was all soft and dark and loamy. He stuck out his best digging paw, then his second best digging paw, and then all four paws were flying.It was wonderful. He'd be able to dig the most ginormous holes in this garden.

For in Frog's experience of digging, and he had a lot of digging experience, some soil just wasn't suitable. There were many reasons soil might be unsuitable for digging: too hard, too rocky, or too wet with clay. But the Jones' garden in the Cynon Valley was just heavenly diggable perfection.

"Wot's he doing?" shouted Miles.

"Diggin' a hole," said Mr Jones, pulling a face. "Don't let your Mam see him doing that."

Mrs Jones was in the kitchen making a pot of tea, happily unaware of the digging that was going on in the garden. Mrs Jones was an easy-going woman on the whole, but if there was one thing she didn't tolerate, it was digging in the garden. The garden was her pride and joy. Mrs Jones and Frog were headed on a collision course if he was going to take up digging.

"Here comes Monster!" squealed Bethan suddenly.

Frog jumped in fright, stopped digging, and swung round, squinting wildly. Coming towards him was the largest, fiercest ball of moth-eaten cat fur he had ever laid eyes upon. Frog felt weak with relief, for Monster was a cat, just a cat. What a lot of fuss about nothing.

Still, he wasn't about to take any chances with Monster, because Monster was a fairly frightening example of cat. And right now Monster was not happy to find a stranger in his garden. He swelled up to twice his regular cat size (which was enormous already) and moved slowly, threateningly, and hissingly towards Frog. Monster was clearly a force to be reckoned with. Frog stepped back hastily. Monster advanced further. Frog did not like the look in Monster's eyes.

"Be nice, Monster," pleaded Mrs Jones from the back door. Mrs Jones liked peace in the home; she wanted everyone to get along. "That's our new doggy friend. He's called Frog and I am sure you and he are going to be the best of friends in no time."

Monster hissed a second time. Monster didn't do nice and Monster didn't do friends. Even the children had to be careful around Monster, because he could turn nasty in a flash. Frog turned tail and waddled quickly to cower behind Mrs Jones' skinny legs.

This show of cowardice pleased Monster. He gave Frog a scornful look as if to say, *"you aren't worth bothering about,"* turned his back and started to wash himself.

"I think they will be all right," said Mrs Jones, "once they have had time to get used to each other."

The pecking order at the Joneses was now crystal clear to Frog. Monster was at the very top, ruling everybody, and he was followed by Mr Jones and Mrs Jones. The three children came next in order of age, and he, Frog, was right at the very bottom. Frog didn't mind being bottom of the pecking order. He'd never been hungry for power. All he'd ever wanted was to be loved and accepted, warts, of which he had quite a few, and all.

Chapter Three

Frog's first outing into the streets of the village was never going to pass by without folk making comments. That's because nothing ever went unnoticed in the village. If someone put up new curtains, everyone would notice and comment. So there was fat chance a new dog would go unnoticed, and certainly not a dog that looked as peculiar as Frog.

Euan, Miles and Bethan were proud and excited to take Frog for his first walk. They squabbled over who would hold the lead. They'd never had a dog before and couldn't wait to show him off to the other kids.

Frog waddled serenely down Valley Ridge Road alongside his new children. Hope for his new life was rising in his doggy breast. It was all going so much better than he had imagined when first he met the Joneses, just a few short hours before.

The picture of a good life was unfolding before him, a life with lots of walks in it, lots of 'smoothing,' and with Love in it. Love was the thing that Frog hungered after more than gravy bones and dog biscuits, even more than soft loamy soil that was perfect for digging.

But Frog's dreams of Love were broken just seconds into his first walk. They'd hardly gone fifty paces when the Gang from No. 10 appeared, as if majicked from thin air by Indian smoke signals.

The Gang from No. 10 had a bad reputation all through the village. Their leader was Joseph Williams the Third, a tough-faced boy of eleven who was all freckles and mouth. It was a mouth that got a lot of exercise and it was a mouth that got Joseph Williams III into a lot of trouble. It was a mouth that had folk saying "You watch your mouth, young man," several times a day.

Being mouthy ran in the Williams family. Joseph's dad had a real mouth on him, and his grandfather had one too. His great grandfather, Joseph Williams the First, had had the biggest mouth of them all.

The only difference between this young Joseph and his great grandfather that anyone could see was that the first Joseph had used his mouth to better effect. He'd used it to lead the miner's strike in 1912 and had become something of a local hero. Young Joseph III had to content himself leading the Gang from No. 10, getting into trouble, and being a hero in no-one's eyes except his own, and those of the other gang members.

"Oy," yelled Joseph Williams III, now spear-heading the Gang from No. 10, like the point of an arrow, with the other members fanned out behind him.They came stomping towards the Jones children and Frog. "Oy, wot you got there? Is it an alien? It looks like an alien. Did you get it from Mars?"

The other members of the Gang from No. 10 laughed long and loud at the wit of their leader, Joseph Williams III.

"He's not an alien," replied Miles with dignity, his spectacles steaming up with panic. Miles was scared of Joseph Williams III and the Gang from No. 10. "He's our new dog. We got him today from the pound in Merthyr Vale."

"He don't look like a dog," replied Joseph Williams III scornfully. "He looks like an alien. Wot's his name?"

"Frog," said Bethan, who hadn't thought there was anything funny about Frog's name until she heard the Gang's reaction.

For the Gang nearly had hysterics when they heard Frog's name. Some of them were bent double they were laughing so hard. Others pointed and crowed and still others called their friends to come and have a laugh as well. Soon all the other kids in the street — even those who weren't members of the Gang — had come along to laugh at the funny dog that looked like a frog, and was even called Frog.

Euan and Miles looked at each other in dismay. They hadn't seen anything wrong with Frog until now. It wasn't very nice looking at their new dog through the eyes of scoffers. He looked different, somehow, uglier, even a bit ridiculous.

Euan was embarrassed and went quiet. He handed the lead back to Miles. "You can walk him now," he said. He wanted to put some distance between himself and Frog.

Frog's new-found confidence was crumbling into bits all around him. He had embarrassed his new children! His flat paddle of a tail sank between his legs, his round shoulders grew even rounder, and his head went down. His squinty eyes were now fixed firmly on the pavement and he tried to make himself as small and invisible as possible.

But Bethan Jones was made of stronger stuff than her brothers. "Take no notice of them," she said to Euan and Miles and to Frog. She glared at the Gang who were still shrieking and folded over with laughter. *She* wasn't bothered by the Gang from No. 10. And besides, she *liked* Frog. Frog was much nicer than Joseph Williams III, who was just a stupid boy who thought he was king of the village.

"Come on," she said stoutly to her brothers. "They're just being stupid. Let's go." And so the Joneses and Frog pushed their way through the Gang from No. 10, turned left at the corner of Valley Ridge Road and made their way down to the river.

The Gang weren't about to give up the joke that easily. They hadn't had this much fun in weeks. So as one they set off to follow the Joneses and Frog, all the while competing to outdo one other with the wit of their jokes.

As the group made its way down the hill, other children from the lower terraced streets joined them, and by the time the procession reached the bridge, most of the village kids were part of the following pack.

All this was very upsetting for the Joneses and it was very upsetting for Frog.

"Alien! It's an Alien. It's not a dog, it's an Alien!" was the cry and the howls of laughter were hard to bear. With each newcomer that joined the party, the noise levels rose.

Bethan was walking as fast as her thin legs would carry her. Miles was upset, and more than a little scared. Euan was torn between rage and embarrassment. But there was no point taking on the Gang when they were in this taunting mob mood. There was nothing for it but to try and ignore the comments and the laughter as best they could, and hope the Gang would get tired of it sooner or later and leave them alone.

The Joneses, Frog and the mob crossed the river over the old metal bridge, and turned left along the paved riverside path on the other side. It was a good path for walking and fishing, lined with overhanging trees that were now in full summer leaf.

The river itself was narrow and dark, and much deeper than it looked. It rose in the heart of the Brecon Beacons and then twisted its way down the valley, passing through the village on its way to join its larger brother, the Taff, from whence the two flowed as one towards Cardiff and the sea.

The Cynon was by no means the prettiest river in Wales. This was not so much the fault of the river as the fault of all the lazy litter bugs who lived in the village. The river banks were scattered with thousands of bits and bobs that had no right to be there at all. There were drink cans and bottles, plastic bags and broken toys. There were even bits of old motor cars and furniture.

When the river rose after rain, as it would do very often, for in Wales it rained often and hard, it would sweep all the litter up with it, and then there'd be bedposts and broomsticks floating downstream, all the way to Cardiff.

"Our new national flower," Mrs Jones used to call the plastic bags and the tin cans.

"Aye, but it's better than it was," Mr Jones would reply, for he always tried to look on the bright side of things. "When the mines were still running, the river was black as coal, and there was no life in it at all. At least the fish are back now, and the ducks. Why, old Billy James swears he's even seen a family of otters wot's arrived to make their home here."

The children knew how bad the valley had been back in the days when the mines were still working. Everything had been black in those days, covered in a layer of coal dust. Even the mountain, now green, had been black in those black days. When the women used to hang out their washing on the line to dry, within minutes it too would black, covered in the coal dust that hung everywhere around the valley. All that had changed for the better when the mines had closed, but some things had changed for the worse. There were few jobs to be found, and lots of people in the village were now very poor.

Coming towards them, also covered in black from head to toe, but not from coal dust, was a plump, middle-aged man and his dog. The Jones children had never been so pleased to see the Vicar before. They'd never had reason to be pleased to see the Vicar before. He was just the not-terribly-interesting man who came and talked at them at school assembly once a week in a fruity and cheerful just-for-children voice.

No-one had ever seen the Vicar wearing anything other than black. He always went out and about in full black clerical clothing and he even wore a black clerical hat like something only ever seen in very old photographs.

"He's very high church, is the Vicar," Mrs Jones always said. "I bet you he wears black pyjamas to bed."

Mr Jones always replied that he would rather not think about the Vicar in his pyjamas.

The children weren't too sure what high church was, but from the way Mrs Jones said it, they could tell it wasn't nearly as good as low church. Being high church seemed to have something to do with candles and bells and with wearing black pyjamas to bed.

"How now, children," said the Vicar to the Joneses in his fruity voice, taking in the situation with a sweeping glance. He noted the mob of following children and all the jeering, the whooping and the whistling. He noted the dog that looked like a frog. "Well, well, what have we here?"

"This is our new dog, called Frog," said Bethan. She wasn't as confident as she had been before. The mob's jeers and the laughter had had their effect.

"Yes, I see," said the Vicar, smiling at Frog and offering him a dog biscuit. Frog's tail stirred. He did enjoy a treat.

"That is a very fine dog you've got there," the Vicar said loudly and admiringly to the Joneses. He said it loudly enough for the whole Gang to hear. "I haven't seen such a fine dog in years."

The Joneses stared in surprise and so did Frog. This was an unexpected turn of events. The Vicar's words also stopped the Gang from No. 10 in their tracks. It hadn't occurred to any of them that Frog might be a fine dog.

"A fine dog?" faltered Joseph Williams III. He respected the opinion of the Vicar, because they'd had a few run-ins in the past, and the Vicar had come out on top every time. Joseph respected anyone capable of getting the better of him, because not many could. But now Joseph Williams III's world view was tottering. He could have sworn Frog was some sort of freak of nature, and not a fine dog at all.

"Oh yes, he's easily the finest Manchurian Mountain Dog I have ever seen in my life," the Vicar continued, very loudly and fruitily. "Very rare, you know, Manchurian Mountain Dogs. Very brave and very rare."

No-one was laughing and jeering now. Everyone was staring at the Manchurian Mountain Dog with new eyes. As for the Jones children, they were quite swollen with pride by the time the Vicar had done praising the fine points of their Manchurian Mountain Dog. How lucky they were to own one.

"I imagine he was very expensive," the Vicar continued, getting into his stride. "I wouldn't be surprised if he wasn't the only Manchurian Mountain Dog in the whole valley, possibly even the whole of Wales."

"We got him from the pound," blurted Miles. "He wasn't expensive at all."

"Then you were very lucky indeed," said the Vicar. "You've got a treasure there. You be sure to look after him very well."

No-one was more astonished by all this than Frog. This was the first he'd heard of his ancestral links to the mountain dogs of Manchuria. Yet as he thought about it, it all started to make sense. Of course that's what he was. No wonder he didn't feel he belonged in Wales, with all the bull-terriers and spaniels and Jack Russell terriers. No, he belonged in Manchuria with the mountain dogs. He could just imagine himself bounding across the mountains of Manchuria, where all the other dogs looked just like him, and were proud to do so.

His round shoulders straightened, his paddle tail emerged from between his legs, where it had been hiding ever since the Gang from No. 10 started mocking him, and his bowed head lifted. Yes, life was suddenly good again — it was good to discover he was a Manchurian Mountain Dog.

The Vicar gave Frog another pat, raised his black hat to the mob of children, and went on his way. Then everyone wanted a turn holding Frog's lead. Bitter fights broke out, because there were too many hands and only one Manchurian Mountain Dog.

"Maybe I'll let you have a turn next time we go for a walk," Euan said to the disappointed many. It felt good to be the owner of the highly sought after Manchurian Mountain Dog. It would gain him a lot of power with the Gang from No. 10.

By the time Frog and the Joneses had climbed the steep hill back to Valley Ridge Road, Frog was puffing and panting, half dead with exhaustion. Cynon Bach was one of the steepest hillside villages in the whole of South Wales and all that sitting around in the pound meant he wasn't very fit.

"Did you have a nice walk with Frog?" Mrs Jones asked when they got back.

The children were all talking at once, brim-full of news and Mr and Mrs Jones couldn't make head or tail of what they were saying at first.

"Frog's a Manchurian Mountain Dog!" blurted Bethan excitedly.

"What?" said Mr Jones with a laugh. "Don't be silly, he's no such thing!"

"Yes he is," insisted Euan, "the Vicar said so, and you should've seen Joseph Williams III's face when the Vicar said how rare and expensive Manchurian Mountain Dogs are."

Mr and Mrs Jones looked at Frog and then at each other. "I am not so sure about that," said Mrs Jones doubtfully. "You'd think they would have known about it at the pound. They said he wasn't any breed at all that they could tell."

"It's true," said Miles, excitedly. "The Vicar said he's probably the only Manchurian Mountain Dog in the whole valley, and maybe even the whole of Wales. The Gang from No. 10 were being really mean and laughing at Frog before the Vicar told them that. It shut them up right away. After that everyone wanted to be friends with Frog — it was wicked!"

Mr and Mrs Jones looked at Frog and then again at each other. "Well, I never," said Mr Jones, winking at Mrs Jones.

"Were those awful children from Number 10 giving you trouble again?" asked Mrs Jones.

"They were laughing at Frog and being mean," said Bethan.

"Take no notice of them," said Mrs Jones. "I am very glad the Vicar put them straight about Frog. He's a good egg is the Vicar. If anyone is likely to know about Manchurian Mountain Dogs it's the Vicar. He's travelled a lot, has the Vicar. He's even been to Russia. Perhaps that's where he learned about Manchurian Mountain Dogs."

Mrs Jones divided the population of the village as if they were types of eggs. There were good eggs — that included the Vicar, the postmaster, Mrs Davies from two doors down, and her own family. Then there were bad eggs — the folk who had regular visits from the community constable, for example. There were hard-boiled eggs, like the folk from Number 10, and there were fragile eggs. Her final category, and this included the next door neighbours on the left, were scrambled eggs. She even had mixed categories, like good scrambled eggs, or bad fragile eggs. At the end of the day, there was no shortage of grades of eggs to describe all the people who lived in the village.

"I made Frog a comfy bed in the corner of the kitchen while you were out," she said now. Frog liked the sound of that a lot. He was tired out from the excitement of the day and his walk by the river. He lumbered downstairs to give it a try.

It wasn't a bad bed, not bad at all. Mrs Jones had cut an old mattress in half and covered it with a spare duvet. It was a lot more comfy than the bed at the pound. He flopped down and squinted gratefully up at Mrs Jones. She smiled back. Mrs Jones liked everyone to be happy and comfortable.

Life's looking up, thought Frog sleepily, as the family bustled about the kitchen around him, getting ready for their tea. Mrs Jones is a nice, kind lady. Mr Jones is a bit loud, but he isn't too bad either. And they are nice children, with nothing mean and nasty about them. Perhaps I haven't done too badly after all, he thought, drifting into a sleep filled with dreams of digging up the Jones' garden, and enjoying all the admiration due to a rare Manchurian Mountain Dog.

Chapter Four

Frog's second day with the Joneses dawned a beautiful day in June. The children were happy because it was Sunday, there was no school, and they had their new Manchurian Mountain Dog to share it with.

Frog was out in the garden early. He had important business to attend to. It was time to make a start on that hole. Soon soil was flying in every direction and all that could be seen of him was his large round behind, bouncing up and down as he worked.

"Stop him!" shrieked Mrs Jones from the kitchen door. "Stop him! He's ruining my flower beds."

Frog stopped. He looked up from his work. Shrieking was a new and unwelcome development. He hoped Mrs Jones wasn't going to make a habit of shrieking every time he worked in the garden.

"Throw a ball for him or something," suggested Mr Jones, who was sitting on the wooden patio reading the Sunday papers. "He'll enjoy that. He's probably just bored."

Humans don't understand a thing, thought Frog. *Not a thing.* Now here was Euan getting ready to toss him an old tennis ball as if it was a treat. There was nothing for it but to stop digging and join in the stupid game of chase, catch and throw. Frog wasn't very good at catching, and he was too large for chasing. Playing ball just wasn't his thing. Still, the children seemed to enjoy it and Frog liked to think of himself as a team player.

Just when he thought they would never tire of the game, a head appeared over the garden fence on the left hand side. It was a shaven head, with coils of snake tattoos on skull, cheek and neck. The face was thin and pale, with a pair of large watery pale green eyes. This was the neighbour Mrs Jones called a 'right scrambled egg.'

The scrambled egg's name was Stefano. It was actually Stephen, but Stephen didn't sound tough enough, so he had renamed himself Stefano. He lived with his wife Belinda, or Bel for short, a plump young woman with bright red dyed hair and not many brains beneath it.

"Orwight?" said Stefano to the Joneses in general, but no-one in particular.

"Orwight," replied Mr Jones without enthusiasm. Mr Jones didn't have much time for Stefano because Stefano had been 'On the Sick' ever since he left school.

The children understood this meant the government paid Stefano money each week to do nothing. Mr Jones got hot under the collar about this, because as far as he could see, there was not much wrong with Stefano that a bit of hard work wouldn't fix.

"There's plenty of folk with lots wrong with them round 'ere," he'd say, "wot struggle off to work each day, if they can find it, and they don't go On the Sick."

Stefano said he was 'On the Sick' because he'd been dropped on his head as a baby, and he'd never been quite right since.

"He just needs to be dropped on his head a second time," Mr Jones would grumble. "That would sort him out."

"Don't say things like that," Mrs Jones would reply, sounding a little shocked. "There's two sides to every story. We don't know their side of it."

The problem with having Stefano and Bel as neighbours — one of the problems, anyway — was they were always short of money. "We're skint till Tuesday," said Stefano now, fixing his face into what he thought was the right expression to go with the state of being skint. He made himself look a little sad and wistful. "Would it be orwight to borrow some washing-up liquid? Bel 'ere ain't got nothing to wash the dishes with."

Mr Jones mumbled something and sighed and went inside to fetch a cup of washing-up liquid. "I don't know why he bothers calling it borrowing," he grumbled to Mrs Jones. "He's never brought back a single thing he's ever borrowed."

"Oy, wot's that you've got there?" called Stefano, taking the cup of washing-up liquid without so much as a thank you, and suddenly noticing Frog.

"That's our new dog. He's called Frog," said Miles.

"Cor, he's ugly," said Stefano pulling a face.

"Not half as ugly as you," muttered Euan under his breath.

"Wot's that?" Stefano asked sharply.

"Nothing," said Euan, "nothing."

"He's a rare Manchurian Mountain Dog," Bethan said proudly, "the only one in the whole of Wales."

"Is that right?" Stefano gave Frog a second, considering look. Frog didn't care too much for the gleam that appeared suddenly in Stefano's eyes. There was something about Stefano Frog didn't like at all.

"So wot's he worth then?" asked Stefano.

"Thousands," said Bethan, "thousands of pounds."

Stefano's watery eyes gleamed more brightly at that and Frog shivered suddenly, as if the sun had gone behind a cloud. He wished Bethan hadn't said that. There are lots of things that should go unsaid in this world, and Frog thought that was one of them.

In the afternoon the Joneses went out in their car. This they did every Sunday, calling to pick up Grandpa Jones on their way. Grandpa Jones lived in the Retirement Home, having moved there when Grandma Jones died, because he could no longer look after himself properly.

"You're late," said Grandpa Jones crossly. He was sitting on a bench outside the Home, his hands curved round the top of his walking stick, waiting. He looked like a much older version of Mr Jones. "I've been waiting for you for hours."

Grandpa Jones was what Mrs Jones called a fragile egg, because he wasn't terribly well and was always moaning. Now he huffed and puffed and moaned about having to share the back seat with three children and Frog. There wasn't enough room, he said.

"Wot you go getting such a *big* dog for?" he complained. No-one took too much notice of Grandpa Jones' moaning and complaining, because he did it all the time and they were used to it. Grandpa Jones had spent twenty years down the coal mines and twenty years breathing in coal dust had done terrible things to his lungs.

"Grandpa Jones is proper poorly," Mrs Jones would say, by way of explanation. "It's only because he's poorly that he's so grumpy. When I first knew him he was always laughing and joking. Poor Grandpa Jones. It's terrible sad, really."

Sometimes the family went to Barry Island and spent the afternoon on the beach there. When there wasn't enough money for petrol, they would go somewhere closer. Today it was Dare Valley Park in Aberdare, where there was lots of space to run about. The young Joneses took a football to kick about and a bag of stale bread for the ducks. The adults took the Sunday papers and a flask of tea.

The children fed the ducks and then tried to get Frog to have a swim in the lake. *There is so much these Joneses don't understand about me*, thought Frog, who, in spite of his name, hated getting wet more than just about anything else.

Then they all sat round on the grass next to the bench where Mr and Mrs Jones and Grandpa were. Mrs Jones had brought along homemade chocolate brownies.

"Don't give any to Frog," she said to the children. "You should never give dogs chocolate. It's bad for them." She'd bought some dog treats instead so Frog wouldn't feel left out.

"Let's have a look at this new dog of yours," said Grandpa Jones, in between slurps of tea. "What sort of dog is he?"

"He's a Manchurian Mountain Dog," said Miles. "He's very rare. The only one in the Valley, possibly in the whole of Wales."

"Whatever makes you think that?" Grandpa Jones asked.

"The Vicar said so."

Grandpa Jones looked at Mrs and Mrs Jones and they winked back at him.

"I wouldn't be surprised to discover he's related to Sir Peking Yangtze, the Manchurian Mountain Dog who lived in this very Valley many, many years ago," mused Grandpa Jones after a thoughtful pause. "Now that was a fine dog, if ever there was. Your Frog has a look of Sir Peking about him," he continued, staring hard at Frog. "Not that I knew Sir Peking meself, of course, but I did see a photograph once."

"Who was Sir Peking Yangtze?" asked Bethan.

"Have I never told you about Sir Peking Yangtze?"

"No, you haven't. Tell us now, please Gramps."

Frog pricked up his ears. He couldn't wait to hear the story either.

"Well, when I was young," Grandpa Jones began, "there was an old man called Lloyd Evans what lived in our street. Many years before he had travelled over the seas to the Far East to make his fortune, but it all went badly for him out there, and when he came home he had nothing to show for it but a Chinese wife and a Manchurian Mountain Dog. The dog was Sir Peking Yangtze, of course.

"Because he was down to his last penny, Lloyd took a job in the mine. It was work in the mine or starve in them days, of course. And it was dangerous in the mines as you know, very dangerous. I don't think there was a single family in the whole Valley wot didn't lose someone in those mines at some time or other. Why, my very own uncle - your great, great uncle Bill - he died down the mines in an explosion."

The children and Frog waited impatiently for Grandpa Jones to get back to the point and eventually he did. "Every morning Lloyd Evans went off to work down the mines. Sir Peking would sit at the front gate all day long waiting for him to come home. I doubt there was a more loyal or devoted dog in the whole of Wales."

Frog stirred proudly.

"Then one day Lloyd didn't come home. There were sirens and bells going off down at the mine and the old fire engine was racing to the scene. Sir Peking was pacing up and down and whining, because he knew something was wrong, and at last he jumped the fence and ran down the hill to search for his master.

"Three miners were trapped in a tunnel, see, and one of 'em was Lloyd. Time was running out. There wasn't much air down there, and if it all got used up, they'd all die, sure as eggs is eggs."

The children were holding their breath, as if air might run out for them as well.

"There was a sideways tunnel into the mountainside, not a downwards one," Grandpa Jones explained. "And Sir Peking Yangtze was into that blocked up tunnel like a flash. No-one had ever seen anything like it. He dug like a machine, only he was faster than any machine. He dug his way into the collapsed tunnel in half the time it would have taken the fire brigade."

"That sounds like our Frog," said Mrs Jones with a smile. "He's good at digging too."

"Runs in the family, then, " said Grandpa Jones. "Anyway, people talked about the way that Manchurian Mountain Dog saved the lives of those men for years."

"They all made it out safely?" asked Mr Jones, carried away by Grandpa Jones' story, in spite of himself.

"They were all half dead, but luckily only *half* dead. That dog was the hero of the village and he was even given a medal for bravery. Lloyd Evans had to take him to Buckingham Palace to get it from the King. And from that day on, wherever he went, people would say: there goes Sir Peking Yangtze, the dog what saved the miners."

Grandpa Jones finished his story triumphantly, and leaned back on the bench, well pleased with his efforts.

"Do you suppose Frog is Sir Peking's great grandson or something?" Miles asked.

"Almost certainly," said Grandpa Jones. "He looks just like him, if the photo I saw is anything to go by."

Frog rested his head on Grandpa Jones' foot, and sighed happily. He had no difficulty at all believing he was great grandson of the great Sir Peking Yangtze, hero of the Cynon Valley.

Chapter Five

In no time at all Frog felt as if he had lived with the Joneses all his life, and he soon grew comfortable with their daily routine. Every day Mr Jones went to work in the factory across the river where they made disposable nappies. And every day the children went to Cynon Bach Primary school, just down the road. After they'd all gone, Mrs Jones would take Frog for a walk around the block and then she'd put him in the garden while she cleaned the house.

Frog spent his time in the garden tiptoeing carefully around Monster. He'd soon learned how important it was not to annoy Monster, because Monster had very sharp claws and was not afraid to use them.

Then, on Wednesdays, Mrs Jones went to Aberdare to do the weekly shopping and this was the only time Frog was left all by himself. He usually seized the chance to do some work on his hole in the garden.

He had to pick his time carefully, because Mrs Jones reacted most excitedly if she caught him working on his hole. She would shriek at the top of her voice and sometimes even throw her shoe at him. Then she'd ruin all his good work by shovelling all the earth he'd dug up straight back into the hole. But the small matter of the hole aside, life was turning out to be unexpectedly perfect with the Joneses.

Frog was a different dog now. He was growing in confidence, and just as Sir Peking Yangtze had waited at the gate for Lloyd Evans to come home from the mines every day, so Frog waited every day at the front door of 20 Valley Ridge Road for his children to come home from school.

They were always very pleased to see him, and there'd be lots of love and cuddles. Then they'd change out of their school uniforms and take him for a walk down by the river.

Thus passed the first month.

But alas there was a storm cloud gathering. It seemed to be coming from next door, for Frog couldn't help noticing that the scrambled egg called Stefano spent an awful lot of time peering at him over the fence, licking his lips, as if he was considering a tasty treat.

The look in Stefano's eyes gave Frog the creeps.

The storm clouds over the fence reached bursting point one Wednesday when Mrs Jones went shopping as usual, leaving Frog in the garden because it was such a lovely day.

"I won't be long," she said from the kitchen door. "Be a good boy, and NO DIGGING."

Frog managed not to dig for a whole ten minutes. He lay on the patio staring at the hole at the bottom of the garden, groaning with the effort of not digging. At last it was just too much. He peeped cautiously over his round left shoulder to make sure Mrs Jones had gone. Yes, the coast was clear. Just a little dig, he promised himself, just a couple of minutes. What possible harm could that do? Soon there was earth flying everywhere in that satisfying way it had, and Frog's hole was deeper than ever.

Then an unexpected movement seen out of the corner of his eye stopped Frog in mid-dig. There was a jeaned leg coming over the fence. It was joined by a second jeaned leg. The legs belonged to Stefano. He climbed the fence, dropped into the Jones' garden and marched towards Frog with a look of cunning in his eye and a leather lead in his hand.

Frog was deeply alarmed. There was something very wrong about this. Stefano was not a Jones and only Joneses had the right to be in the garden, marching towards him with a lead in their hands.

"Oy, dog, come here," snarled Stefano.

Frog retreated to the far corner of the garden, but Stefano kept coming. There was nowhere to escape. Frog was all wedged up against the fence. He tried to duck, but it was no use. Stefano clipped the lead to his collar and started dragging him towards the back garden gate.

The Joneses never used the back garden gate. It was always bolted and secure and had been that way ever since Frog arrived. It led onto a narrow, overgrown alleyway that ran between the houses of Valley Ridge Road and the back gardens of the next street down.

Stefano had to struggle with the bolt, which was rusty and stiff, and it took him a few tries to get it open. Then, with a vicious yank, he dragged Frog into the alleyway behind him. Frog sat down hard on his large round behind. He didn't want to go for a walk with Stefano. The Joneses didn't like Stefano, and anyone the Joneses didn't like, Frog did not like either. On principle.

But while Stefano may have been thin and weedy-looking, he was in truth tough and strong, and Frog found himself being scraped and bumped along the alleyway on his behind. At the end of the alley Stefano's wife Bel was waiting, all dressed up in a tight skirt, high heels, with her bright red hair piled on top of her head in a retro bouffant-style. She had lots of thick make-up plastered all over her face.

She looked nervous and worried. "Oh Babe," she said to Stefano, "Are you sure we ought to be doing this? It doesn't seem right."

"Oh Babe," echoed Stefano nastily, in a high-pitched mocking voice. "Oh Babe. You're the Baby. Didn't you hear what the Joneses said? He's worth thousands. Think what we could do with thousands. We could have a holiday in Spain with thousands."

"Yes, but the Joneses will be so upset...!"

"I'll buy you that new washing machine you're always nagging me about and then you won't have to keep asking Mrs Jones to do our washing. So we'd be doing them a favour, see?"

"Yes, I suppose so," Bel agreed doubtfully as they turned down the hill. She teetered along on her high heels a few paces behind Stefano and Frog.

Frog didn't like the sound of any of this one little bit. He sat down again heavily, dug in his paws and used his great weight to stop himself being taken on this horrible walk he didn't want to go on. Stefano snarled and aimed a sharp kick to Frog's plump behind. Frog yelped and got up again hurriedly.

Perhaps this is not the best time to be a hero, he thought. He tried to think what Sir Peking Yangtze would do, but his mind went a complete blank and it seemed there was nothing for it, but to do everything Stefano wanted.

Stefano and Bel kept glancing nervously to left and right as they dragged Frog down the hill towards the village. They kept to the quieter side streets away from the village centre because they didn't want anyone to see them.

Frog's heart sank when he saw the train station ahead. They were going somewhere on the train and soon there'd be no hope of giving Stefano and Bel the slip.

Frog had never been on a train, and when it pulled into Cynon Bach station, he decided he didn't much want to either. Now here was a monster worthy of the name.He made one last bid for freedom. He jerked backwards and almost managed to slip his collar. Unfortunately his neck was so thick with folds of fur and flesh, the collar stayed fast and all he got for his pains was another sharp kick in the behind from Stefano. So poor Frog found himself on the train southbound for Cardiff, shackled by collar and lead to the unlovely Stefano.

"What's your dog's name?" asked the train conductor, patting Frog kindly on the head.

I'm not his dog! I'm not his dog! I'm not his dog! screamed Frog silently. *I've been dognapped. Help!*

"Mind your own business," Stefano said rudely to the conductor.

"Some people!" shrugged the conductor, moving on down the carriage, with a sympathetic glance at Frog.

The train rumbled down the valley, stopping at all the small village stations along the way, and then, in no time at all they'd reached the outer suburbs of Cardiff. Minutes later they were in the noisy station that was Cardiff Central.

"This is our stop," said Stefano, tugging sharply at Frog's lead. Because Stefano had booted all the fight out of him, Frog waddled along miserably beside the pair through the busy streets. Stefano was jerking him roughly every few yards and telling him to "Get a move on."

Then they stopped. They were standing outside an enormous shop in the middle of a shopping mall. The name on the sign read *Posh Pets of Cardiff*.

"This is the place," said Stefano. "The biggest pet shop in Wales. I looked it up on the internet."

Frog had never seen anything like it. *Posh Pets of Cardiff* had rows of glass tanks full of exotic fish from all over the world, alleys of bird cages squawk full of colourful tropical birds all the colours of the rainbow, and dozens of puppy and kitten cages with expensive price tags and certificates of pedigree.

Stefano and Bel dragged him to the counter where stood a posh young man in a shiny pin-striped suit. He had a badge on his lapel that read "Assistant Manager – Richard."

"Wot'll you give me for this rare Manchurian Mountain Dog?" Stefano asked abruptly.

Posh Richard was startled. He peered at Frog for a long moment, and then his lips twitched, as if he was trying hard not to laugh.

"I am very sorry, sir," said Posh Richard, politely, but firmly. "There is no such thing as a Manchurian Mountain Dog. The dog you have here is an ordinary mixed breed. He's got a bit of everything in him, I suspect, but Manchurian Mountain Dog he is not. Of course we don't buy mixed breed dogs here — there's no demand for them."

It would have been hard to say who was more disappointed, Frog or Stefano. Frog had just had the most wonderful month of his life as a Manchurian Mountain Dog. It was unbearable to think about going back to being just a plain mixed breed without a proper name, just unbearable.

"You're making a big mistake, mate," said Stefano, trying to keep the panic out of his voice. "Everybody in our village knows this is a Manchurian Mountain Dog."

But Posh Richard wasn't having any of it. "I am very sorry sir," he kept repeating, "there's no such thing," until Stefano had no choice but to accept he wasn't going to leave *Posh Pets of Cardiff* a wealthy man.

"And to think I went to the trouble of hacking into the Jones' broadband connection, just so I could look up holidays in Spain on the internet!" he muttered to Bel. "It took me blinkin' hours."

With the holiday in Spain melting away, Stefano started to get angry. Most of his anger was aimed at Frog, and what was left was aimed at the Joneses.

"Come on, Bel," he said. "Let's get out of here. We've been had. Those Joneses were just having a laugh. I've never been so done over in all my life. It shouldn't be allowed — people telling lies about their dogs like that. Manchurian Mountain Dog, my eye. Stupid mongrel, more like."

"What about the dog?" asked Bel.

"What about him? He's more trouble than he's worth," Stefano said, grabbing Bel's arm and making for the door.

"We can't just leave him here," protested Bel.

"You can't just leave him here!" protested Posh Richard.

"Just watch me," said Stefano, pulling poor protesting Bel behind him. She wobbled dangerously on her high heels, but Stefano broke into a jog and they disappeared out of the pet shop and into the crowded mall.

Richard ran after them to the door. Frog didn't move an inch. He didn't want to spend one more second with Stefano and Bel. He'd had more than enough of them already.

Richard gave up. He couldn't very well leave the shop unattended, and go chasing after Stefano and Bel through the streets of Cardiff. He came back inside and stared at Frog with a worried frown. "What am I going to do with you?" he said, but not unkindly.

Frog's shoulders sank, his tail went between his legs, and he stared at the ground. He wanted to be home with the Joneses, not abandoned in a posh pet shop in Cardiff with rows of squawking parrots and mewling kittens. Why, he might even end up back in the pound. After his wonderful month as a Manchurian Mountain Dog with a family who loved him, the thought of going back to the animal shelter in Merthyr Vale was more than he could bear. He sat down and began to cry.

Posh Richard felt sorry for him "Never mind, big boy," he said in a kind voice. "You'll be all right. I'll find out where you come from and get you home safely." He put Frog in one of the larger dog cages, with food and water, and a sign that said *Not For Sale*, and went into the back office to Make Inquiries.

Back in Valley Ridge Road all was confusion and panic. Mrs Jones had returned from shopping to find an empty garden, and a garden gate swinging open in the breeze. Her heart froze and her breath caught in her throat. It was a terrible, terrible moment.

She knew the gate had been bolted when she went out. No-one in the family ever used the back gate. There was only one possible explanation. Frog had been stolen. But that was nonsense — why would anyone want to steal Frog?

They wouldn't, of course they wouldn't. Then a little thought started to niggle at the back of her mind, like a buried clue that wouldn't go away. No-one would want to steal Frog, of course not, but someone *might* want to steal a Manchurian Mountain Dog.

Mrs Jones rang Mr Jones at the factory. She hadn't been this upset since Grandma Jones died. "Don't worry, Lovely," said Mr Jones comfortingly. "I'll come home from work early and sort this out. It's probably just the Gang from No. 10 playing a joke."

"He's been stolen," wailed Mrs Jones. "I know he has. Call the police! We have to find him before the children come home from school. They'll be heart-broken."

Mr Jones was there in minutes and immediately rang the community constable. Soon everyone in the street was twitching their net curtains and peeking and peering to see what was going on at the Joneses. It was always more interesting than the television when the police came calling on someone in the street.

And this was a real surprise too, because it was the Joneses the police were visiting. The Joneses never ever had visits from the police. It was usually the Williamses at No. 10, or Marty Dodge and his mates at No. 31, the ones who wore their baseball caps backwards and got up to goodness knows what, who had visits from the police.

Mr and Mrs Jones were far too upset to care what anyone thought. "Someone stole our dog," cried Mrs Jones to the community constable. "I'll show you where they made their getaway." She led him downstairs and showed him the back gate in the fence, still swinging open in the summer breeze.

"Now why would anyone want to steal your dog, Mrs Jones?" The constable was wearing the sort of reassuring smile people wear when they aren't taking things seriously. "I am sure he is a very nice dog, but no-one would go to the trouble of stealing him. You probably just left your gate unlocked, and your dog took himself off for a walk. He'll be back in time for his tea, he will."

The gate was never unlocked, Mrs Jones protested. Frog had surely been stolen. "The Vicar said Frog was a Manchurian Mountain Dog, you see, and now everyone thinks he's worth thousands of pounds."

"Ah, I do see," said the constable. "That's a very useful piece of information, Mrs Jones, very useful indeed. If someone stole your dog, my guess is they will try and sell him in Pontypridd or Aberdare or maybe even Cardiff. I'll make some inquiries. Don't you worry now, we'll have your...er.. Manchurian Mountain Dog back in no time at all."

Mrs Jones felt better knowing the community constable was on the case. But, oh, the sorrow of the young Joneses when they came home from school was unbearably great. Bethan began to cry and Miles fought hard not to join her. Euan went white-faced and serious and stood silently, wringing his hands.

"Why don't you go and look for him," suggested Mr Jones. "Perhaps he is just out having a walk." He didn't believe it, because he knew how stiff the bolt on the back gate was, but he thought it might help the children if they had something to do.

So the three changed out of their school uniforms and went in search of Frog. Joseph Williams III and some of the gang were sitting on the steps of Number 10 when they hurried past.

"Oy," called out Joseph Williams III. "Where's your Manchurian Mountain Dog, then?"

"He's been stolen," wept Bethan. "We're going to look for him."

"Stolen?" yelled Joseph Williams III, in a voice of rage and thunder. Any suspicion the Jones children might have had that the Gang from No. 10 had anything to do with Frog's disappearance vanished in an instant.

Joseph Williams III was suddenly a man with a mission. It was for crises such as these that he had been born. He whistled the Urgent Rallying Call to summon the rest of the Gang and in seconds they were all there, gathered about, and ready for action.

"Red Alert," said Joseph Williams III. "It's a Red Alert situation. Some plonker has stolen the Mountain Dog from the Joneses. They're not gonna get away with it, not if I have anything to do with it."

The Gang murmured in agreement. Everyone felt they owned a piece of Frog now. Hadn't they been the first to welcome him to the Valley? Hadn't they been first to recognize his true worth?

Joseph Williams III organized his gang with all the skill of a military general. "You take the river path to the north," he said to the Joneses. "Make sure you go as far as the railway bridge and back. Me and this lot will go south, and then loop back on the mountainside. The small ones can check the football field and the park. Has each team got a watch? Good. Report back here in an hour."

It was wasted effort, of course, because Frog was at that moment miles away, whimpering quietly to himself in a cage in *Posh Pets of Cardiff*, contemplating the terribleness of a life without Love.

So it was a tired and disappointed army of children that returned to the appointed spot an hour later. "He's probably in England by now," said Joseph Williams III. "You'll probably never see him again."

The Joneses were all very sad that evening. Miles couldn't face his dinner and even Monster looked a little lost, as if he knew something was wrong. Monster quite enjoyed having Frog in the house. It was fun creeping up and hissing in Frog's ear just for the fun of seeing him jump.

As the day faded, and just as they were about to give up all hope, there came a knock on the door. Mr Jones sprang up from the couch, where the whole family was huddled and cuddled together, watching *The Cube* to take their minds off the missingness of Frog.

Standing at the door was the community constable. In his left hand he had a lead and at the end of the lead was Frog. Frog's squat paddle of a tail was swirling like a propeller and his round face all slobbering smiles. He was delirious with joy at seeing his family again.

"We've found your Manchurian Mountain Dog," the community constable said with a grin. "He was in Cardiff. A young couple took him to a pet shop and tried to sell him. They thought he was worth thousands, it seems."

The Jones children flung themselves at Frog and soon the living room floor was a tangle of arms and legs and paws.

"A young couple, eh?" said Mr Jones. "And what did this young couple look like, then?"

"The young man was thin, with tattoos and pale green eyes. The young woman was large with dyed red hair. Or so the fellow at the pet shop said."

"Well I never! Stefano and Bel," cried Mrs Jones, "our neighbours on the left! Who would have thought it? What a cheek! And to think only yesterday Stefano borrowed money for trainfare to Cardiff. He said his aunty was sick and he had to go and visit her, and I believed him."

"Indeed," said the community constable. "Indeed it was great cheek. But don't worry, Mrs Jones, I'm just off right now to take them down to the station for a little chat."

The whole street, including the Joneses, left their televisions to watch through their net curtains as Stefano and Bel were bundled into the police van, off to the station for a little chat.

"Serve them right," said Mr Jones.

"What will happen to them?" asked Euan.

"Dunno," said Mr Jones," but you can bet they won't go round stealing other people's Manchurian Mountain Dogs again in a hurry."

"They might even stop coming round borrowing things for a while," said Mrs Jones hopefully, but deep down she didn't really think that was likely. There was no end to the cheek of Stefano and Bel, not that she'd ever discovered.

"Is Frog really not a Manchurian Mountain Dog after all?" asked Bethan, who'd started putting two and two together and was busy coming up with four.

"Of course he is," Mrs Jones assured her. "Of course he is. He's our very own rare and valuable Manchurian Mountain Dog — the only one in the valley, possibly the only one in the whole of Wales."

Frog was now thoroughly confused. He'd started the day as a Manchurian Mountain Dog. In Cardiff he had gone back to being a mongrel, and now he was a Manchurian Mountain Dog again. It was impossible to understand humans. No point even trying. But oh, it was good to be back in his bed, to be surrounded by Love, and to put the whole dreadful business behind him.

The dog-napping incident did have some positive results. It changed Frog's relationship with the Joneses for one thing. They'd all been getting along very nicely before it happened, but nearly losing him made them all even closer.

And then the whole village got behind Frog and the Joneses. Everyone had a kind word to say.

"It's a Valleys thing," said Mrs Jones proudly. "We Valleys folk stick together because we're all in the same leaky boat and we've always been in the same leaky boat, right from the start."

Best of all, Stefano and Bel moved out of the house next door just a few days later. They slipped away in the middle of the night.

"They've done a moonlight flit," said Mr Jones. People were always doing moonlight flits in the Valley when they got in trouble with the police or owed lots of money to the debt collectors. They'd just pack up and disappear without telling anyone where they were going.

Mrs Jones thought this particular moonlight flit was because Stefano and Bel were embarrassed about the whole Frog-napping business. Everyone in the village knew what they had done, and Stefano wasn't able to show his face in the betting shop without being jeered at. Poor Bel, whose fault it wasn't really, couldn't show her face at the hairdressers or the supermarket either.

There was a rumour they'd moved over the hill to Tonypandy and Mrs Jones said she felt sorry for their new neighbours there. Then she felt bad about saying that. She also felt bad about wanting to throw a great big party to celebrate the fact that they'd gone.

So all in all the whole episode did no harm to Frog's position in the village. And even though there were rumours he wasn't really a Manchurian Mountain Dog after all, most people preferred to think he was.

There was even a short article in the Cynon Clarion, with the headline *Dog Thieves Foiled* and a nice blurry shot of Frog looking happy, surrounded by happy and proud Joneses. This caused the Gang from No. 10 to adopt him as their mascot and Joseph Williams III gave Euan a tiny skull and crossbones to hang on his collar.

Chapter Six

June had come and gone, and so too July, which for Frog passed in a blur of walks and Love. Then came the day everyone had been waiting for. That day was, of course, the last day of term, and the start of the summer holidays. There were to be no lessons, and, as a special treat, the head-teacher, Miss Parker, had announced an all-morning concert.

The children divided into groups and each group prepared a short play to put on for all the others. The show took place in the school hall and any parents who weren't working were invited. Lots of parents came and the hall was packed.

The show got off with a real bang. First up was the Gang from No. 10. Joseph Williams III had had a wonderful idea. It would be fun, he had decided, to do a scene from *The Great Train Robbery*. Some of the Gang members were playing the part of passengers on the imaginary train, while Joseph Williams III and a couple of others were playing the part of the train robbers. Everything was going very well, and the audience was cheering and whooping.

Then Joseph Williams III reached into the case he was carrying and pulled out his dad's new airgun. He had thought it wasn't possible to do a play about a robbery without a decent gun, as anyone with any sense would agree. But Miss Parker and the rest of the staff and parents didn't agree at all.

"Stop!" screamed Miss Parker, leaping from her chair and thundering up onto the stage. "Give me that gun AT ONCE. Have you completely lost your mind, boy?"

Joseph Williams stopped short in the act of aiming the air gun at the imaginary train and stared open mouthed back at Miss Parker.

"It's not loaded," he said.

"I don't care if it's loaded or not," she shrieked. "Give it to me at once."

"Won't," said Joseph Williams III, putting the air gun behind his back.

"Yes, you will."

"Won't," said Joseph Williams III. "You can't make me."

"Oh yes I can," said Miss Parker. And of course she could, although it took a bit of doing, and she needed help from some of the dads in the audience before she managed it.

"You've wrecked our play," said Joseph Williams III sulkily, as he and his gang stood gunless about the stage. "We can't do a proper play about a robbery without a gun."

"Nonsense," said Miss Parker briskly. "We'll find you something else to use as a gun."

Someone found a piece of wood that was about the right shape for a gun. Joseph Williams III thought it was a very poor exchange for the real thing, but he didn't have any choice and the show went on. In spite of not having a proper gun, at the end of it there were lots of dead bodies all over the stage and the audience found that very entertaining. The applause was so enthusiastic, in fact, that Joseph Williams III even stopped looking sulky and cross.

But the triumph of the day was without doubt the play put on by the Joneses. Theirs was the final performance and while there'd been lots of other good plays in between, none had really lived up to the Great Train Robbery. It was hard to compete with dead bodies all over the stage.

The Joneses brought Frog on the stage to act out the story of Sir Peking Yangtze and the mine rescue. Euan played the part of Lloyd Evans, and Bethan looked very sweet in a little Chinese costume, playing his wife.

(She'd kicked up a real fuss beforehand about having to play Euan's wife, though."Who'd want to be Euan's wife? Yuck," she'd said.)

There wasn't a proper part for Miles, so he pretended to be one of the firemen. Frog was there too, pretending to dig a tunnel on the stage. The children had spent a week training him to do it and he'd picked it up really quickly, because he was a very smart dog, was Frog. The story went down a treat with the audience, because just about everyone there had lost some or other great grandfather or great uncle to a disaster in the mines back in the olden days. It went down so well, everyone stood up to cheer and clap.

"What is your dog's name?" asked Miss Parker, climbing up onto the stage to bring the show to a close and declare the holidays started.

"Frog," said Euan.

"I think you should call him something nicer than that," she said. "He's such a clever dog and Frog is an ugly name. Why don't you call him the Frog Prince instead?"

The Joneses liked that idea, and so did Frog. Then the bell rang for the start of the holidays, and the Joneses raced home with their Frog Prince, full of joy at the thought of all those weeks of freedom to come.

@@@

It was a glorious summer, the best Frog had ever known. Every morning he and the children got up early, and went down to the river with their fishing rods and their bucket of stinky bait.

"Will we have trout for supper tonight?" Mrs Jones would ask each time with a smile, but they never caught a thing, except for plastic bags and tin cans. Still, fishing was fun even if they didn't catch anything.

Through the long, warm summer evenings, the Joneses, Frog and Monster would sit out on the patio and Mr Jones would barbecue budget sausages bought from the supermarket, and they'd all wish it was trout.

Then one evening the weather turned. By dusk great rolls of thunder rumbled through the valley. By dark great jagged streaks of lightning ripped across the sullen sky. There was no barbecue on the patio that night, and the stars of the valley were hidden behind thick black clouds.

Frog was terrified. He hated thunderstorms even more than he hated being bathed. He tried to squeeze under Bethan's bed where Monster was already cowering and trembling and looking nothing at all like the Monster everyone tiptoed around in fear. Then the heavens opened and the rain poured out, and it drummed down on the roof all night long. Mr Jones put a bucket in the corner of the boys' bedroom where the roof leaked a little and in the morning the bucket was overflowing.

But the sun was out again and the sky was all new-washed and clean. It was as if the storm had never been. The children gathered their fishing rods and their bucket of bait and trooped as usual to the front door after breakfast.

"Be careful," Mrs Jones called after them. "The river will be up today."

"We will, we will," they called back impatiently, wondering why she always made such a fuss about everything.

Before they got to the bridge they could hear the river roaring. The day before it had been little more than a sluggish creek. Now it was swollen with rain — up at least ten feet and thundering through the narrow ravine, crashing about the rocks, and carrying great branches in its swirls and eddies. The children had never seen it so high or so violent.

"Look at that!" exclaimed Euan with a whistle. "It must have rained buckets in the night."

"It did," said Miles. "We've got a bucket in our bedroom to prove it."

Their normal fishing spot, a flat rock large enough for all of them to sit on, was nowhere to be seen, so deep was it sunk beneath the swirling torrent. It took a while to find somewhere else that was suitable. At last Euan spotted a cluster of rocks jutting out over the foaming waters. They would have to sit on one apiece, and put their gear on the fourth.

"That'll do," he said.

The rocks were wet and slippery with spray from the river that was roaring by a few inches below. The children made their way carefully down the bank and stepped gingerly onto the rocks. Miles set the bait and their sandwiches down on the empty rock next to him and sat down to bait his hook.

Frog hung back on the river path and wandered up and down, snuffling at all the fresh new smells the rain had brought out of the earth. He wasn't planning on going anywhere near that noisy raging torrent. No sir. He had more brains than that.

"Pass the bait," said Euan to Miles, threading a new hook on the end of his line, because he'd quickly lost his first one to some submerged rocks. "I don't know we'll catch anything today," he said doubtfully. "I think the river needs to be a bit quieter to have any hopes of catching anything."

"We never catch anything, anyway," said Bethan a little scornfully, "so what's the difference?"

"You are just a girl, you don't know nothing," said Euan crossly.

"I know lots more than you," she replied heatedly and they started to argue so fiercely neither noticed what was happening to Miles.

Miles leaned across the rock beside him for the bucket of bait. It was just out of reach of his fingers. He leaned a bit further, but it was still an inch too far away. He stood up, and keeping one foot on the rock he'd been sitting on, stretched the other across the gap and placed it gingerly on the rock with the bucket of bait.

His foot landed on a tuft of moss, all slimy and slippery from the recent drenching. One second Miles was teetering between the two rocks, the next he was gone. His foot slipped and into the river he went, swept away by the raging current. Euan and Bethan could see his head bobbing up and down, his eyes wide with terror. In a flash he was ten yards away, then he was twenty, and in no time at all he was fifty yards downstream.

Bethan opened her mouth and screamed at the top of her voice.

Frog did not stop to think. One of his children was in trouble. He launched himself at the river. The shock of the cold water took his breath away. The current carried him along at the same hurtling pace as Miles. He could see Miles ahead of him, and he used his large well-formed digging paws as paddles to catch up.

Because Miles was trying to swim against the current, and because Frog was swimming with the current, the gap between the two closed quickly. Then Frog was alongside Miles. Using all the loyalty and devotion that he had been practicing, he dived under the water and offered his back and his neck to Miles as if he was a surfboard. Miles flung both arms round Frog's broad neck and hung on as if his life depended on it.

Frog took the brunt of the pressure of the water. His body was pounded by rocks and branches, and all the other debris that the storm had swept into the swirling river. He turned to the bank, and started to paddle hard towards it, using every ounce of strength he had.

Euan and Bethan were running down the bank alongside the pair in the water. Suddenly the Vicar was there too, with that strange habit he had of turning up at desperately important moments.

"Frog, Frog," Bethan was screaming, "this way, this way."

The Vicar snapped a branch from a nearby tree and scrambled down as close to the swirling water's edge as he dared. He held the branch out to Miles.

"Grab onto this, son," he yelled, "grab onto this."

Miles let go of Frog and lunged for the branch. He just managed to get a hand on it before the water swept him away again. It was one of those moments that could have gone either way. If he'd missed the branch it would have been all over.

The Vicar heaved the branch towards the bank and as soon as Miles was close enough, grabbed him by the shirt, and dragged him coughing and spluttering onto the bank.

When they saw Miles was safe, Euan and Bethan turned to help Frog. He had used up all his strength rescuing Miles and he was getting weaker. His head disappeared beneath the surface as the current dragged him down. When he struggled up for air, his eyes were rolling about. Euan managed to grab hold of his collar, and Bethan grabbed hold of Euan's belt so he didn't end up in the water as well.

Suddenly more help was on the scene. Mr Morgan from the fish and chip shop was also out with his dog and he helped Eauan and Bethan drag poor half-drowned Frog from the water. Then the Vicar carried Miles, all limp and dripping and shivering, while Mr Morgan and Euan carried Frog, and the whole party stumbled back up the hill to Valley Ridge Road.

Poor Mrs Jones had the shock of her life. She was cleaning her front window all the better to keep an eye on the goings-on in the street, and was admiring the effects of windowlene and sunshine on sparkly clean glass, when she saw the terrible procession coming towards the house. She gave a cry and dropped her cloth and ran to the front door.

"Miles," she shrieked. "Oh Miles, are you all right?"

"Don't worry, Mrs Jones, he's fine," the Vicar reassured her. "He just had a little dip in the river. He's wet, and he's shocked, but he's going to be fine."

"Frog saved him," Bethan was saying over and over. "Frog saved Miles from drowning. Frog saved Miles."

Mrs Jones rushed for dry clothes and a warm blanket for Miles, and made him a cup of hot cocoa. Then the Vicar helped Mr Morgan carry Frog downstairs to his bed in the kitchen. His little squinty eyes were shut and he was scarcely breathing.

"Oh poor Frog," cried Bethan. "He's badly hurt. Wake up Frog."

"He's probably just tired," said the Vicar in his fruity cheerful voice.

Frog did not look at all well, and he wasn't. He scarcely moved for hours. Long after Miles was well enough to run around the garden with Euan in chase of a ball, Frog lay still on his bed, moaning and sighing quietly to himself.

Bethan stayed with him, stroking his head gently. "Please get better, Frog," she said. "Please get better."

"I suppose we should take him to the vet," said Mr Jones when he came home from work.

Mrs Jones knew how much vets cost. If they took Frog to the vet there wouldn't be enough money for food and electricity for the rest of the week. "Yes, I suppose we'd better," she said, looking even more worried than usual.

The vet looked very serious after he'd examined Frog. "I have to be truthful with you," he said. "It's going to be touch and go. He seems to have done some serious damage to his insides from bashing up against the rocks in the river. I don't know if he is going to make it. Would you like to leave him here overnight, so we can keep an eye on him?"

"No!" cried Bethan loudly, and everyone turned to stare at her. "He must come home with us," she wailed. "Please, Mam, please Da, please, don't leave Frog here, he'll be so unhappy. We have to have him home with us."

The vet nodded. "He will be happier at home, it is true."

With the week's housekeeping money gone, and a packet of painkillers to ease Frog's suffering, the Joneses drove home, and together they heaved him back down the stairs to his bed.

`Bethan made a camp beside him. She got her duvet and her pillow from her bed and put them on the kitchen floor and begged Mrs Jones to let her spend the night there with him.

"There's nothing you can do for him, Babes. He probably just needs to sleep."

"I don't want him to be lonely and sad when he wakes up," said Bethan stubbornly, and at last Mrs Jones agreed.

Then the house went still and quiet and everyone slept except Bethan. She kept thinking about Miles swept away by the raging current. The terrible scene played over and over in her mind. She couldn't stop thinking about the way poor dear Frog, who hated water, had gone straight in and saved her brother, without any thought to his own safety.

It was hours before she fell asleep at last, curled up on her duvet on the kitchen floor next to Frog's still body, her hand resting lightly on his back.

Much later in the night Frog stirred, and his stirring woke Bethan. He was struggling to his feet. He lumbered to the back door, whimpering. Bethan felt hot prickly tears of sympathy welling up.

"What's the matter, Froggy? Do you want to go out?" She struggled with the lock on the back door and when she got it open, Frog crawled out onto the patio, where he collapsed again, as exhausted as if he'd just run a marathon.

The night sky above was starry and clear. A great sickle moon hung low in the sky, and the stars of the valley seemed even brighter than usual. Bethan lay down on the patio beside Frog and wrapped her arms about his neck.

"Please don't die, Froggy. I love you. We all love you. We don't want you to go." Her tears splashed all over his head.

Then she saw that the dark back garden had started to glow with a soft light, as if someone had turned on some outdoor lighting. Frog stirred. He struggled to his feet, and stood up.

He seemed stronger all of a sudden and looked almost handsome, doglike, and not froglike. And Bethan saw the light in the garden was coming from inside Frog himself. His whole body was glowing. She gazed in wonder as the light gradually started to rise upwards into the air, just a little bit at first, hovering over the patio, and then gathering speed as it rose higher and higher into the night sky.

The light was now all gathered into a ball, like one of those helium balloons people let off after parties, getting smaller and smaller as it rose higher and higher. At last it was just a small pinprick in the night, no bigger than one of the stars that shone over the valley.

Everything suddenly went dark. Bethan blinked her eyes and rubbed them and looked about. She was alone in the garden.

"Mam, Da," she cried, running back through the dark house and up the stairs to the bedrooms on the top floor. "Come quickly, Frog's gone!"

"Whaaat?" grumbled Mr Jones sleepily. "What are you talking about, Bethan? Where's he gone?"

"He's gone, I tell you, he's gone."

Mr Jones was wide awake now, and so was Mrs Jones. Bethan's yelling had woken the boys as well. All the Joneses put on their dressing gowns and went downstairs and out onto the patio.

"Oh," wept Mrs Jones, "Oh no. Poor Frog."

Miles and Euan also started to cry. Even Mr Jones was fighting back tears. For there, on the patio, lay the still body of their dear Frog Prince. " I am so sorry, children. Our poor Frog is dead," said Mrs Jones. "He gave his life for Miles. We owe him everything."

"You don't understand!" said Bethan impatiently. "He's not dead, he's just gone."

"It was all just too much for the poor dog, Babes. He is dead, I'm afraid."

"No, he isn't," insisted Bethan. "He's up there." She pointed to where the stars of the valley twinkled brightly above. "I watched him go home. I watched him float off into the sky. He was happy. I know he was. He wouldn't want us to cry. He let me watch him go home, so we wouldn't be too sad."

Mr and Mrs Jones looked at each other over her head. "Panadol," said Mrs Jones firmly. "Its all been too much for her too, poor little thing."

Bethan tried to explain, but it was no use. They hadn't been there and they hadn't seen what she had seen. Miles believed her, though. She could tell from the way he was looking at her. But then Miles had also had a very special moment with Frog in the river. He knew how incredible Frog was.

"He was a hero," said Miles.

"He was *our* hero," agreed Mr Jones. "We were so very blessed to know him. Go back to bed, children. I'll bury him in that great big hole he dug at the bottom of the garden. It seems the right place for him."

"Unselfish to the last," said Mrs Jones. "To think he even dug his own grave. It's almost as if he *knew* he was going to die and wanted to save us having to bother over all that. To think I shouted at him and threw shoes at him because of that hole. But how was I to know?"

The children didn't want to go back to bed. They wanted to help bury Frog and say their goodbyes properly.

"We could say a little prayer, or something," said Mr Jones.

"I know, we'll read a psalm," said Mrs Jones, and went to fetch Grandma Jones' old Bible which had been used as a doorstop in the upstairs loo for as long as anyone could remember.

It took her quite a while to find the right psalm, with just the faltering beam of Mr Jones' flashlight to help her.

"Yea, though I walk through the valley of the shadow of death, I will fear no evil, for though art with me...." Mrs Jones read aloud in a quavering voice, "Good bye dear Frog. God bless."

"Goodbye Frog," echoed everyone, the boys in tears.

Young Bethan Jones was the only one not crying, for she knew Frog wasn't really dead. She knew he'd gone to join Sir Peking Yangtze and all the other Manchurian Mountain Dogs in that faraway place where all the dogs looked just like him, and where it was perfectly fine to look that way. No, Frog wasn't dead. He'd just gone home, that's all.

The End

Other titles in the Animals of the Valley Series:

Bird King Spring
Animal Ark Autumn
Magic Fish Winter

To find out more about the *Animals of the Valley* series, including pictures of the valley where the books are set, visit
http://books.wordwinnower.com/children

10256221R00045

Printed in Great Britain
by Amazon.co.uk, Ltd.,
Marston Gate.